HEIDI HECKELBECK

for Class President

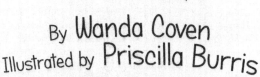

By Wanda Coven
Illustrated by Priscilla Burris

LITTLE SIMON
New York London Toronto Sydney New Delhi

LITTLE SIMON
An imprint of Simon & Schuster Children's Publishing Division
1230 Avenue of the Americas, New York, New York 10020
First Little Simon paperback edition August 2020
Copyright © 2020 by Simon & Schuster, Inc.
Also available in a Little Simon hardcover edition.
All rights reserved, including the right of reproduction in whole
or in part in any form. LITTLE SIMON is a registered trademark
of Simon & Schuster, Inc., and associated colophon is a trademark
of Simon & Schuster, Inc. For information about special discounts for bulk
purchases, please contact Simon & Schuster Special Sales at 1-866-506-1949
or business@simonandschuster.com. The Simon & Schuster Speakers Bureau
can bring authors to your live event. For more information or to book an event
contact the Simon & Schuster Speakers Bureau at 1-866-248-3049 or visit our
website at www.simonspeakers.com.
Designed by Ciara Gay
Manufactured in the United States of America 0720 MTN
10 9 8 7 6 5 4 3 2 1
This book has been cataloged with the Library of Congress.
ISBN 978-1-5344-6131-4 (hc)
ISBN 978-1-5344-6130-7 (pbk)
ISBN 978-1-5344-6132-1 (eBook)

CONTENTS

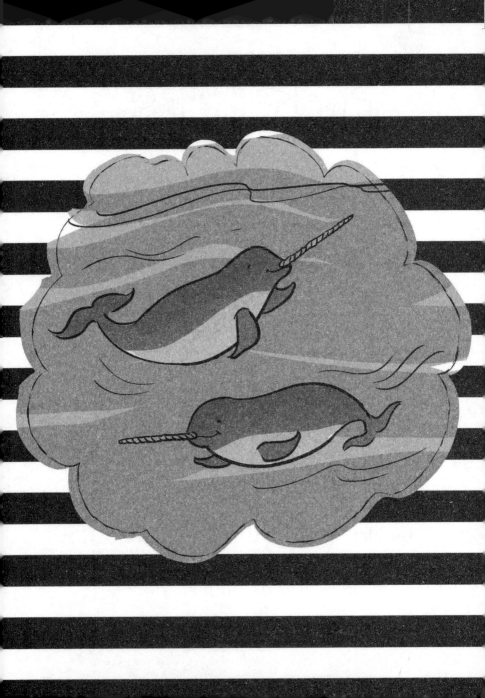

SPLOOSH!

Heidi Heckelbeck and Bruce Bickerson talked about narwhals the whole way to school.

"Narwhals are the unicorns of the sea!" Heidi said as the two friends hopped off the bus. "And they grant wishes with their magical horns!"

Heidi loved these mysterious whales with the single spiral tusk.

Bruce looked at Heidi as if *she* had a horn. He was a scientist, and scientists love facts.

"There are so many things wrong with that statement," Bruce declared. "First of all, it's not a horn. It's a tooth that grows out of the narwhal's lip.

Second, the tooth cannot grant wishes, because the tooth is not magical. Third, and most important, there is no such thing as magic."

Heidi giggled, because of course there was such a thing as magic. She practiced magic all the time! But she couldn't exactly tell Bruce she was a witch.

"Okay," she challenged, "if you're such a great scientist, how can you say magic doesn't exist until you prove it doesn't exist?"

Bruce laughed loudly, and Heidi was so busy watching him, she forgot to look where she was going.

Sploosh!

She stepped right into a deep puddle. Cold water filled one of her sneakers.

Heidi hopped back quickly, but the wet muck still seeped into her tights.

"GROSS!" she cried. "Now what am I going to do?!"

Bruce smirked. "Maybe some magic would dry out that soggy sneaker."

Heidi rolled her eyes. "Very funny."

Bruce nudged his friend's shoulder. Then he pointed at the side of the school building.

"See that drainpipe?" he asked. "If that spout were directed behind the bushes rather than at the sidewalk, there wouldn't even have been a puddle to step in."

Heidi sighed heavily. "So what you're saying is, science could've helped me?"

Bruce nodded. "Yeah, but I'm also sorry your day started off on the wrong foot."

Heidi looked down at her wet shoe.

"Me too!"

Chapter 2

CLASS PRESiDENT

Squish!

Squish!

Squish!

Heidi and her squishy shoe made the mistake of walking by Melanie Maplethorpe's desk.

"Oh no," Melanie said with a laugh.

"Heidi, wearing a wet kitchen sponge instead of a shoe is a bold fashion choice. Everyone, look at Heidi's shoe!"

Heidi hurried over to her desk and made a scrunchy face at Melanie.

Then her best friend Lucy Lancaster leaned over and whispered, "What's with your shoe?"

Heidi rolled her eyes and told Lucy about the evil puddle outside.

Lucy frowned. "That's terrible!" she said while scooching closer to Heidi. "I have a funny story that might make you feel better. Want to hear it?"

Heidi nodded— anything to get her mind off her clammy shoe.

"One time, before school, I dribbled maple syrup on my shirt," said Lucy.

"Um, I sure hope there's more to this story," said Heidi.

Lucy giggled. "Well, I didn't notice the syrup at all until I got to school and I bumped into Carter Collins. Like, I bumped into him hard!

The syrup made our shirts stick together! It was so embarrassing!"

Heidi let out a snorty laugh. Lucy could always make her feel better. Maybe one day Heidi would be able to laugh about her soggy shoe story too. But not today.

At the front of the room Mrs. Welli rang her silver bell.

"Hello, students!" the teacher sang cheerily. "We have a surprise guest this morning, who has a very special announcement."

Principal Pennypacker walked into the room. He had on a gray suit and black loafers. He placed his hands behind his back and cleared his throat.

"Greetings, class!" he said. "I'm here to talk about the upcoming school election."

All the kids murmured with excitement.

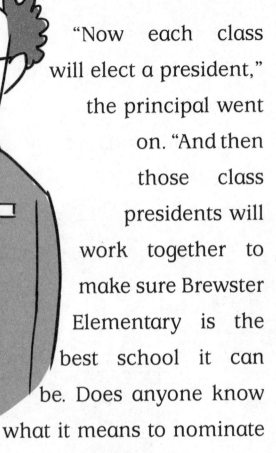

"Now each class will elect a president," the principal went on. "And then those class presidents will work together to make sure Brewster Elementary is the best school it can be. Does anyone know what it means to nominate a candidate in an election?"

Stanley Stonewrecker's hand shot up quickly.

"I do!" he said. "It's when you name somebody YOU think would make a good candidate. And a candidate is someone who runs for office, like the office of president."

Principal Pennypacker smiled and said, "That's exactly right! Anyone who would like to run for president must be nominated by a fellow student. Then the candidates must

show the voters what they would do
if they were elected president. At the
end of the week, each class will vote.
Are there any questions?"

Laurel Lambert raised her hand.
"Um, can anybody in the class be
nominated?"

Principal Pennypacker nodded. "Yes, Laurel!"

Charlie Chen also waved his hand. "Does the president get to ride in a limo?"

The principal chuckled. "Sorry, no limos. If there aren't any other questions, then I'll see you on election day!"

Nobody else raised a hand, so the principal moved on to the next classroom.

Heidi sighed and rested her chin
on the palms of her hands. *Hmm,
I wonder if I would make a good
president,* she thought.

Chapter 3

DOWN WiTH PUDDLES!

The class broke into small groups to talk about the election. Heidi sat in a group with Lucy, Bruce, Laurel, and Stanley.

"So, Bruce, what would YOU do if you were voted class president?" Heidi asked her friend.

Bruce sat on the edge of his chair and said, "That's EASY! I would build a state-of-the-art laboratory, where students could invent cool stuff—maybe even cure the common cold!"

Then Heidi turned to Lucy. "How about you?"

Lucy tilted her head to one side. "I would add more nonfiction books to the library. Also, I would take our class on a field trip to the Chocolate Chunkery Candy Factory. The factory has an indoor roller coaster, and they hand out FREE chocolate bars!"

Without waiting for Heidi to ask her, Laurel announced, "If I were class president, students could bring their pets to school EVERY day. Then we'd get to play with our furry friends at recess."

Stanley pretended to be a dog barking excitedly. "Woof, I'd vote for pets at school! Woof! But if I were class president, I would also make sure pizza was on the menu EVERY day."

Mrs. Welli laughed. She had been listening to all their ideas. "I'm not sure a class president would get to make those kinds of decisions—even though they sound like fun."

Heidi agreed with her teacher. Fancy laboratories and visits to chocolate factories did seem a little out of reach. She tapped her pencil against her lips.

"Well, if I were president," Heidi started, "the first thing I'd do is get rid of that yucky puddle by the entrance to the school. Bruce says all we'd have to do is redirect the drainpipe to empty behind the bushes. Then the bushes would get watered, not our feet!"

Heidi lifted her soggy shoe off the
ground. "Down with puddles!" she
cried.

Her friends laughed and cheered
for Heidi's idea.

Because *nobody* likes soggy shoes.

Chapter 4

NOMiNEES

Mrs. Welli made the class switch groups to talk about the election.

This time Heidi sat with Eve Etsy, Carter Collins, Natalie Newman, and Melanie, who didn't wait for anyone to ask her what she would do as president.

"When you elect me, I'll put on a school fashion show," Melanie bragged. "Everybody will dress up, and then one person will be crowned Brewster's Most Fashionable."

Heidi actually loved the idea of a fashion show, even though Melanie

would faint if someone other than her won. Melanie already seemed to be imagining herself as Brewster's Top Model.

"That's a really cool idea," Heidi said, trying to be supportive. "Eve, what if you were president?"

Eve grabbed the underside of her chair with both hands. "Well!" she began. "I would definitely get new instruments for the music room. The tambourines are missing jingles, and I can never find a mallet for the xylophone."

Eve looked at Carter, who was sitting next to her.

"Music's cool," he said as he looked around the table, "but I happen to know one thing every class needs more of, and that's recess. Am I right?"

Everybody nodded and cheered a very loud, "Yeeeessss!"

"Then just call me the president of recess!" Carter said.

Heidi gave Carter a thumbs-up and turned to Natalie. "Do you have presidential plans?"

Natalie's cheeks turned bright pink. "Not really," she said, looking down at the floor. "I'm not even sure I want the job."

Heidi smiled. "That's okay. Being president isn't for everyone."

Then Mrs. Welli rapped her gavel on her desk, and everyone looked up from their seats.

"Time to nominate candidates!"
she said. "Now remember, if you are
elected, you will represent our entire
class. It will be a position of hard
work—so if someone nominates you,
make sure this is something you are
willing to do."

The class all nodded.

Mrs. Welli smiled and said, "The floor is now open for nominations."

Lucy's hand shot up first. "I nominate Heidi Heckelbeck!"

Heidi froze as the class cheered. A wave of excitement washed over her.

"Do you accept the nomination, Heidi?" Mrs. Welli asked.

"I accept!" she answered proudly.

Then someone else raised their hand. It was Stanley. "I nominate Melanie Maplethorpe!"

Melanie leaped out of her chair immediately. "I'm SO honored!" she said, bowing in every direction.

Now the whole class cheered for
Melanie—even Heidi.

When everyone quieted down,
Laurel raised her hand. "I would like
to nominate Carter
Collins," she said.

The students
really erupted.
Everybody liked
Carter. He was
one of the nicest
kids at Brewster.

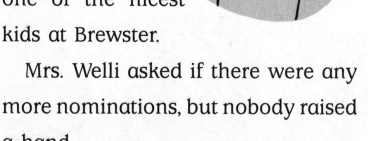

Mrs. Welli asked if there were any
more nominations, but nobody raised
a hand.

"Our stage is set!" Mrs. Welli said. "Would Heidi, Melanie, and Carter please stand as our candidates for class president?"

Heidi stood up, and the kids around her clapped loudly.

Wow! she thought. *I'm a REAL presidential candidate! Well, a real class presidential candidate . . . wearing one very soggy, squishy shoe.*

Merg.

Chapter 5

POSTER CHILD

After school Heidi burst through the back door, followed closely behind by Lucy, Bruce, and her little brother, Henry.

"MOM! DAD! WHERE ARE YOU? I have REALLY BIG NEWS!" Heidi called out through the house.

Mom walked out of the pantry with a packet of lemonade mix. Dad opened the door of his lab.

"What is all the yelling about?" Dad asked.

"Heidi has big news!" said Mom. "Everybody, take a seat at the table, and I'll get some snacks."

The kids all sat down as Mom emptied a bag of popcorn into a bowl.

Everybody took some.

"Are you ready?" Heidi asked.

"Not yet," said Dad as he swiped a piece of popcorn, tossed it in the air, and caught it in his mouth. "Now I'm ready."

"Me too!" Mom said.

Heidi stood up. "SO, my big news IS . . ." She paused to let the excitement build. "Lucy nominated ME for class president!"

Mom and Dad both clapped their hands.

"What an honor!" Mom said. "How many kids are running?"

Heidi counted on three fingers. "Melanie, Carter, and me."

"Oh, Carter is the best, hands down," said Henry. "I mean, no offense, Heidi, but Carter is great. He reads to my class once a week."

Heidi rolled her eyes and grabbed a handful of popcorn.

"Well, fortunately, I don't need your vote, Henry," she said. "This election is for our class only."

"Speaking of, we should make campaign posters," suggested Bruce.

"Good idea! Mom, may we work at the kitchen table?" Heidi asked.

"Of course!" Mom said as she stirred a pitcher of lemonade for the group.

Heidi ran to the art cupboard and pulled out markers, paints, and poster board. She set everything on the table.

"Okay, now we can come up with some catchy campaign slogans!" said Lucy.

Everyone thought for a moment, and then Bruce picked up the saltshaker and held it like a microphone. He began to sing "The Star-Spangled Banner," only with different words . . . and off-key.

"Oh, say can you SEE? Please vote for HEIDI!"

"Hmm, it might sound better on a poster, though," Henry said with a smile.

This made everyone laugh, even Bruce. "I think you're right. Now let's really get to work."

The kitchen was quiet as the kids worked on their posters.

Lucy drew a picture of Heidi's face on hers. Then she stuck a fake mustache on it.

Heidi raised an eyebrow. "What's with the mustache, Lucy?"

"You'll see," said Lucy as she wrote something under the picture.

Heidi read it out loud. "'I mustache you to vote for Heidi Heckelbeck!'"

"Get it?" Lucy asked. 'I mustache you'—as in, 'I must ask you'—to vote for Heidi."

"It's perfect!" said Heidi.

The friends continued working on their posters all afternoon. When Heidi was done, she held up her poster so her friends could see.

It said HEIDI HECKELBECK HAS THE MAGIC TOUCH! VOTE HEIDI ON FRIDAY!

She had used lots of glitter to make the poster look magical.

Heidi Heckelbeck has the MAGIC TOUCH! VOTE HEIDI on Friday!

"That's awesome!" Lucy said.

Bruce agreed. "I bet you'll win!"

Heidi smiled at her friends as she held up another poster.

"Thanks," she said. "I'll do my BEST!"

Chapter 6

ONE TOUGH COOKIE

The next morning Heidi, Carter, and Melanie hung their posters at school.

Carter's had cool slogans like:

VOTE FOR CARTER! HE'S WAY SMARTER!

And . . .

FOR LONGER RECESS EVERY DAY, VOTE FOR CARTER ON ELECTION DAY!

Melanie's posters all had glossy photos of her taped to them. She posed as a cheerleader, a judge, and even a mermaid in the pictures. Plus, she autographed every one of them with a heart dotting the *i*.

Not that Heidi cared. She had work to do. She finished hanging all her posters and returned to her classroom.

Time to let my posters work their magic! she thought.

The rest of the class was busy working on an election worksheet, but then Mrs. Welli clapped her hands.

"Okay, everybody!" she said. "It's time to get to know your presidential candidates.

Please walk around, read the posters, and ask your candidates questions!"

Heidi stayed at her desk and waited for her classmates to come talk with her. But nobody stopped by. Everyone wandered into the hallway.

Heidi got up to join them.

Students crowded the hall, talking to one another and reading posters.

Heidi felt a little silly standing there alone, so she headed for the water fountain.

There was a poster above the fountain that read:

FREE DRINKS ON ME! VOTE FOR CARTER.

Heidi giggled and took a quick drink. Then she headed down the hall where a big table had been set up. All the kids were stopping there.

Along the way there were more Melanie posters. One was taped to a mirror. When Heidi looked at her reflection, it seemed like Melanie was standing right next to her! The poster read:

Heidi had to admit it was a really great poster.

As she approached the table, Heidi wiggled her way to the front and her mouth dropped open. Melanie and Stanley were handing out *free* cookies!

"Have a MAPLEthorpe victory cookie!" said Melanie, handing a treat to Heidi. "The maple flavor will remind you to vote MAPLEthorpe!"

Heidi stared at the cookie and then back at Melanie. "You can't BUY people's votes!"

Melanie gave a shrug and handed Principal Pennypacker a cookie.

The principal held his cookie in front of Heidi. "Cookies are fine," he explained. "They're a wonderful way to make a candidate stand out!"

Heidi sighed. Then she chomped angrily on her cookie.

It was soft, chewy, and absolutely delicious.

Oh, MERG IT ALL! she thought. *Why does Melanie's cookie have to taste SO GOOD?!*

Heidi snuck another bite before throwing the treat away. One thing was for sure: Melanie Maplethorpe was going to be one tough cookie to beat.

Chapter 7

PEP TALK

At dinner Heidi twirled her spaghetti for a very long time.

"How's the campaign trail?" Mom asked. "Were your posters a big hit? I'm sure they were with all that glitter."

Heidi sighed and lifted her fork.

"My posters were fine," she said.

"But Melanie handed out cookies, and everybody loved them."

Henry finished slurping up his spaghetti and said, "Oh, I had one! Best cookie EVER."

Heidi dropped her fork. It clanked on the edge of her bowl.

"EXACTLY," she complained. "How am I supposed to beat THE BEST COOKIES EVER?"

Henry waved his hand at Heidi to get her attention. "That's easy!" he said. "Just promise everyone in your class straight A's! Then you'll get ALL the votes."

Dad laughed. "Giving out cookies—or better grades—doesn't make a good class president," he reminded them.

"Well, it does if you're voting for best-tasting cookies!" Henry said with a fake cough.

"That's true!" Dad announced with a wink. "But since Heidi is running for class president, she needs her *ideas* to reach voters. Will you be able to give a speech?"

Heidi just nodded glumly and said, "We have to give one short speech."

Dad snapped his fingers. "There's your chance!" he said. "A speech allows you to talk about how you can make a difference. Show your classmates how you plan to solve class problems. That is what voters really care about."

Heidi sat up in her chair. She had a little twinge of hope. *Maybe Dad's right. Maybe I CAN make a difference.*

Chapter 8

A PRESiDENT VOiCE

The rest of the week went by quickly, and soon Heidi was in her room, staring at a blank piece of paper. She needed to write her speech for the next day.

Heidi scribbled down a first sentence and read it out loud.

"'Hi, I'm Heidi Heckelbeck, and if I am voted class president, I will solve ALL our school problems.'"

No, scratch that, she thought. *I sound WAY too powerful.* She rewrote the end of the sentence.

"'I'll help our problems go away.'"

Heidi crossed that out too and wondered, *What exactly are the school's problems, anyway?*

Aside from the drainpipe that needed to be moved, Heidi couldn't think of any. She frowned. *How am I supposed to write a winning speech if I don't even know what to talk about? Hmm, this calls for a little magic!*

Heidi stood up from her desk and slid her *Book of Spells* out from under the bed. She studied the chapters and found the perfect spell.

How to Have a Presidential Voice

Have you been nominated for president of a club, a class, or a business? Perhaps you're wondering what to say to your voters? If you want to be a good leader and have a presidential voice, then this is the spell for you!

Ingredients:

1 dash of sugar

1 light bulb

1 organizer

1 paper heart

Mix the ingredients together in a bowl. Hold your Witches of Westwick medallion over your heart. Chant the following spell:

LEADERS HAVE AN OPEN MIND,
LISTENING EARS, AND THOUGHTS
THAT ARE KIND.
TO LISTEN IS A LEADER'S CHOICE.
WHEN YOU DO,
YOU'LL FIND YOUR VOICE.

Heidi collected the ingredients in a large bowl. Then she held her medallion over her heart and chanted the spell. Sparkles swirled and lifted Heidi right off the floor. Then she gently drifted back down.

Heidi hopped to her feet and ran back to her desk to work on the speech. She sat there until bedtime, but oddly, not one idea came to her. Perhaps this spell was a *dud*!

Chapter 9

SPEECH! SPEECH!

The next morning Heidi woke up to an odd sound.

A small plane buzzed in the sky over her house. Heidi looked out the window and saw something trailing behind the plane.

It was a banner!

VOTE FOR MELANIE MAPLETHORPE! was written in giant red letters fluttering over the town.

Heidi rushed to get ready for school. There was no time to lose. She grabbed her backpack and a granola bar, and then ran straight to the bus stop.

Bryce Beltran, Heidi's neighbor, was also early that morning.

"Oh my gosh, Heidi! Did you see Melanie's cool banner?" Bryce asked.

Heidi didn't really know what to say, but that didn't matter. Because when Heidi opened her mouth to answer Bryce, nothing came out. Her voice was gone!

Heidi touched her throat and thought, *Merg! How am I going to give my speech if I've lost my voice?*

Bryce stared at Heidi. "Are you okay? Oh wait, you must be saving your voice for your big speech today."

Heidi nodded—because that's all she could do.

Luckily, Bryce was great at talking, so she let Heidi rest her voice for the whole bus ride.

At school students were watching the plane with Melanie's banner circle in the sky. It was the only thing kids were talking about. At least, until Melanie arrived to hand out even more of her famous cookies.

Heidi wanted to scream, but she couldn't! So instead, she stormed off to class.

VOTE FOR MELANIE MAPLETHORPE!

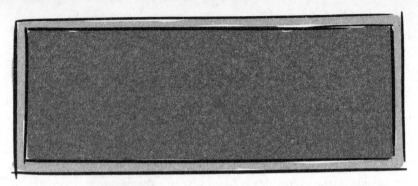

Mrs. Welli had set up a podium and three chairs at the front of the room. As the rest of the class entered, the candidates took their seats by the podium.

"Welcome to the class presidential election!" Mrs. Welli announced. "Our candidates will each have five minutes to speak. When the speeches are done, students will cast their votes. Melanie, you may go first."

Melanie's blond hair swished back and forth as she pranced to the podium. She waited politely for her classmates to stop clapping.

"Hi, everyone! As you all know, MY name is Melanie Maplethorpe, and I'm here to say it would be a TREAT to be your class president. So remember to vote sweet! Vote for Melanie!"

The class cheered, but when the applause died down, the classroom became quiet. Everyone waited for Melanie to say more, but Melanie just stood there.

Soon it began to get uncomfortable, and Mrs. Welli  had to step in. "Melanie, do you have a speech prepared?" she asked.

Melanie simply shook her head. "No. That's all I wrote," she said. Then Melanie held up a tub of cookies. "Would anyone like another cookie?"

But nobody did.

"Um, thank you, Melanie," said Mrs. Welli. "Now let's hear from Carter."

The kids cheered again, and Carter waved to his classmates as he stepped up to the podium.

"Hey, I'm Carter Collins," he said with a smile. "If I were elected to be class president, we would have the best foods at lunch every week: cheesesteak subs, hot dogs, and pizza.

And since I love kickball, I would make sure we have a ton of kickballs on the playground. And, of course, if you vote for ME, you'll get A TON more recess. So vote for CARTER!"

The class whistled, clapped, and cheered.

Heidi clapped too, but she thought Carter's speech only covered what HE wanted. Other kids looked like they felt the same way.

Now it was Heidi's turn. She peeked into her notebook. Had a speech magically appeared?

Nope. There was only one word written on the page:

LISTEN

Suddenly Heidi knew what she had to do.

She didn't go to the podium. Instead, she moved her chair to sit with the class. Then she took a deep breath and tested her voice.

"My name is Heidi Heckelbeck, and I don't want to talk about me. I want to listen to you, my classmates. What would YOU do to make our school a better place?"

The words flowed out of her, and now Heidi waited for her class to respond.

Bruce raised his hand. "We really need new lab equipment," he said.

Heidi thanked Bruce for sharing and called on Stanley.

"The swings on the playground are rusty and squeaky. They need to be cleaned."

Heidi thanked Stanley for pointing this out. Then she called on Laurel.

"The water fountain is too strong, and the water goes up my nose when I drink," she said.

Everyone laughed, even Mrs. Welli, who then signaled that Heidi's time was almost up.

"Thank you all for sharing your ideas with me," said Heidi. "If I'm elected class president, I promise to always listen to you and help in any way I can."

The class whistled and cheered for Heidi.

Mrs. Welli stood in front of the class and said, "Our candidates have spoken! Now it's time to vote!"

All the candidates were listed in alphabetical order on the ballot.

"Mark your choice for president," Mrs. Welli instructed. "Then drop your ballot into the ballot box."

Mrs. Welli held up the ballot box for everyone to see.

It had red-and-white stripes on the sides and a blue lid with white stars. On top was a small rectangular opening. This was where all the kids would place their ballots.

"Vote here!" she said and pointed to the opening.

Everyone in class studied their ballots. Heidi circled her name and folded her ballot in half.

She could hear others marking their votes as she dropped her ballot into the box and returned to her seat.

When all the votes were in, Mrs. Welli handed the ballot box to Principal Pennypacker. The principal left the room with the box. He was the official ballot counter.

The students whispered to one another while they waited. Everyone wondered who would win.

Heidi watched the clock. It was so slow!

Finally Principal Pennypacker returned to the classroom, and the whispering stopped.

"Well, it was a very close race," the principal said. "Are you ready to hear the results?"

"YEEEESSS!" the class cried.

He handed an envelope to their teacher. Mrs. Welli unsealed it and pulled out a slip of paper.

"The winner of the presidential election is . . . Heidi Heckelbeck!"

The class erupted—even Carter and Melanie cheered for Heidi.

Mrs. Welli invited Heidi to stand in front of the class. "Congratulations, Heidi! Is there anything you'd like to say as the new class president?"

Heidi nodded. "First, thank you so much for electing me!" she began. "Thank you to the other candidates, too. Carter had some really cool ideas, and Melanie made everything look and taste amazing. As your class president, I would like to ask Carter and Melanie to work with me."

Carter and Melanie looked at each other and then back at Heidi.

"We're IN!" they said at the same time.

Now the students went wild! And, as Heidi looked at her class, she promised herself she would be the best president Brewster Elementary had ever seen.

Check out the next book starring

HEIDI HECKELBECK

Heidi snuggled under a blanket with her new book, *Jolly Roger, the Pirate Puppy*. This little hound sailed the seven seas in search of buried treasure. Heidi wondered what it would be like to sail with a pirate puppy and dig up treasure.

Then Heidi heard a shriek of

An excerpt from Heidi Heckelbeck and the Hair Emergency!

laughter and dropped her book on the floor. She sat up on the sofa and looked around. *HENRY!*

Heidi shouted in her best pirate voice, "Aaargh! What be the problem, little brother?"

Henry paid no attention to his sister. He was too busy chasing something around the family room.

Heidi rolled onto her side to see what it was. Henry's new wind-up toy—the Roly-Poly Puppy—sped and spun around in circles. This puppy had wheels instead of stubby puppy legs . . . and it was fast.

An excerpt from *Heidi Heckelbeck and the Hair Emergency!*

Henry picked the puppy up and set it down on the floor. He pulled back on the body to wind up the wheels. Then Henry let the toy go.

That Roly-Poly Puppy zoomed all over the carpet. Plus, every time it bumped into something, it giggled, turned around, and took off again in another direction.

Bonk! It bumped into the leg of a chair. *Hee-Hee! Heedle! Heedle! Hee!*

Then the puppy turned and charged into the game cabinet. *Bonk! Hee-hee! Heedle! Heedle! Hee!*

An excerpt from *Heidi Heckelbeck and the Hair Emergency!*